The Party Diaries

Awesome Orange Birthday

written by
Mitali Banerjee Ruths

art by
Aaliya Jaleel

BRANCHES
SCHOLASTIC INC.

W9-BYD-297

For my Adventure Buddies: Drex, Sonya, Leena, Jubby,
Tux—and all the wonderful aunties in my life —MBR

For Fatma, the Melissa to my Priya —AJ

Text copyright © 2023 by Mitali Banerjee Ruths
Art copyright © 2023 by Aaliya Jaleel

All rights reserved. Published by Scholastic Inc., *Publishers since 1920.* SCHOLASTIC,
BRANCHES, and associated logos are trademarks and/or registered trademarks of
Scholastic Inc.

The publisher does not have any control over and does not assume any
responsibility for author or third-party websites or their content.

No part of this publication may be reproduced, stored in a retrieval system, or transmitted in any form
or by any means, electronic, mechanical, photocopying, recording, or otherwise, without written
permission of the publisher. For information regarding permission, write to Scholastic Inc., Attention:
Permissions Department, 557 Broadway, New York, NY 10012.

This book is a work of fiction. Names, characters, places, and incidents are either the product of the
author's imagination or are used fictitiously, and any resemblance to actual persons, living or dead,
business establishments, events, or locales is entirely coincidental.

Library of Congress Cataloging-in-Publication Data

Names: Ruths, Mitali Banerjee, author. | Jaleel, Aaliya, illustrator.
Title: Awesome orange birthday / written by Mitali Banerjee Ruths ;
   illustrated by Aaliya Jaleel.
Description: First edition. | New York : Scholastic Inc., 2023. | Series: The party diaries ; 1 | Audience:
Ages 5–7. | Audience: Grades K–2. | Summary: Priya Chakraborty plans a birthday party for her first
client, Layla Aunty, personalizing everything from the invitations to the menu in Aunty's favorite color,
but as party time finally arrives, Priya is nervous something will go wrong.
Identifiers: LCCN 2021033710 (print) | ISBN 9781338799613 (paperback)
ISBN 9781338799620 (library binding)
Subjects: CYAC: Parties—Fiction. | Birthdays—Fiction. | East Indian Americans—Fiction.
Classification: LCC PZ7.1.R9 Aw 2023 (print) | DDC
   [Fic]—dc23
LC record available at https://lccn.loc.gov/2021033710

10 9 8 7 6 5 4 3 2 1   23 24 25 26 27

Printed in China   62
First edition, January 2023

Edited by Katie Carella
Book design by Maria Mercado

TABLE OF CONTENTS

VIP LIST

(Very Important People)

Samir
(My little brother, also known as Sammy)

Priya
(Me!)

Baba
(My dad, also known as Ashok)

Dida
(My grandmother is my mom's mom.)

Ma
(My mom, also known as Reeta)

Melissa
(My best friend)

Padma Aunty

Susan Aunty

Layla Aunty
(My mom's best friend)

Neda Aunty

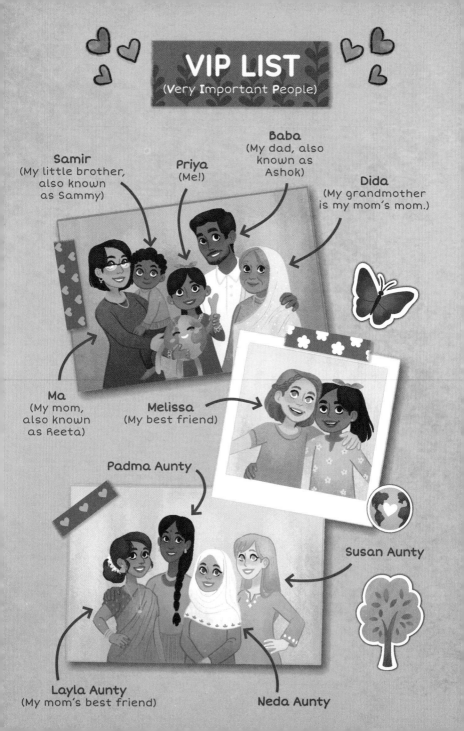

START-UP

Monday

Hello, world! This is my party diary. I write down all my ideas for parties in here.

You see, I just started my own business. It's called:

PRIYA'S PARTIES

My name is Priya Chakraborty. You say it like *pree-ya chuck-ruh-burr-tee.*

Let me tell you about me.

WHAT ANNOYS ME?

Sammy messing up
stuff I organized

The teacher saying
"Miss Chuckerbutty"
(and Ethan Jackman
laughing about it)

People not picking up
their trash

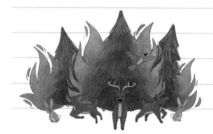

Animal homes
getting destroyed

WHAT MAKES ME HAPPY?

Being with my best friend, Melissa (She lives next door, so I see her a lot.)

Making **DIY** crafts
(Do-It-Yourself)

Quokkas! (They are seriously the cutest animals on the planet.)

Starting my own business to help the planet AND make people happy

Here's how I started Priya's Parties . . .

My mom let me have a
PRIVATE social media account.
That means only friends and
family can see what I post
online.

The first things I posted were pictures of
Sammy's birthday party. My parents were busy
with work, so I made the decorations. I even
baked the cake (with help from Dida)!

DIY party hat

shiny
bottle caps

cardboard
three

paper dinosaurs

Layla Aunty saw my pictures. Then she asked me the BIG question.

I had to say yes because Layla Aunty is my mom's best friend. And because:

WHY QUOKKAS ARE SPECIAL

Quokkas live in Western Australia.

They're related to kangaroos.

You say their name like *kwah-kuh!*

Sometimes they're called the "world's happiest animal" because they're always smiling.

Quokkas are in trouble. If they become extinct, there will be no more quokkas on Earth! That would be a very, very, very sad day.

So that's how my business started.

Now I have to focus on planning Layla Aunty's party. I can work on it every day after school this week.

HOW I'M FEELING

Excited! I get to plan a party!

Worried! Layla Aunty might not like it.

Anxious! There's so much work to do! Will I finish everything in time?

MY FIRST CLIENT

Layla Aunty is my very first client! (That means she hired my business.) So I have to make sure her party is extra special!

I'm coming up with party-planning rules I can follow so every party turns out AWESOME.

Know the Host Rule:

Think about the client!

Her favorite color is **orange.**

She wears orange saris.

She wears orange lipstick.

She has an orange sofa in her living room!

Oh! What if I plan an ORANGE party?!

We could have Layla Aunty's favorite orange snack foods at the party!

- **chevdo (chev-doh):** Like a spicy cereal mix. It's really good!

cornflakes

chili   nuts

- **samosas (su-moh-sahs):** Tasty fried triangles with a crispy crust, usually stuffed with potatoes!

Could we fill the samosas with pumpkin?! Then the insides would be orange.

- **jalebi (juh-lay-bee):** Spirally, crunchy, sticky, sweet fried dough!

- **mango lassi (luh-see):** Basically a fruit smoothie made with mangoes and yogurt!

Dida said to write her a list of what food to make for the party. She's my first employee. (But I don't pay her, so I guess she's actually a volunteer.)

Dida, can you make samosas? It's for a good cause!

Sure, if I have a helper . . .

I like to help Dida in the kitchen. Sammy likes to help, too. He can mix the chevdo, but he'll probably make a mess. He's still figuring out how to control his arms.

PARTY PLANNING

Wednesday

This diary is super useful.

I can write down all the things I need to do. That way, I won't forget anything.

That just gave me a great idea!

Plan Smart Rule:

Make a to-do list!

Now that I have my own business, I want to be professional. That means I have to figure out what I need to do. Then I have to get it done in time for Layla Aunty's Awesome Orange Birthday!

A to-do list can help me plan ahead, stay on track, and feel good. When I finish one of my jobs, I can cross it off the list.

Layla Aunty's Party To-Do List:

♡ Make and deliver invitations.

♡ Make DIY decorations.

I have a really good idea!

♡ Make Layla Aunty's present.

♡ Make snacks.

Even though Layla Aunty ASKED me to throw her a party, she doesn't know what I'm planning. So everything will be a surprise.

THE THING ABOUT SURPRISES

Some people love surprises.

Some people SOMETIMES love surprises.

Sammy loved opening presents on his birthday.

He did not like finding cauliflower in Ma's mac and cheese.

Some people don't like surprises at all.

I don't like surprises. They make me nervous.

I like knowing what to expect ahead of time.

I know all of Layla Aunty's friends will come to the party. (Because they're also my mom's friends.)

Party Guests:

Padma Aunty

Neda Aunty

Ma

Susan Aunty

They might look like quiet ladies. But when all five of them (including Layla Aunty!) get together, they are actually a wild bunch . . .

They set off the sprinklers in a hotel at an Indian wedding.

They painted an elephant at the zoo. (Don't worry! They had permission and everything was safe.)

They drove a golf cart into a lake.

Anyway, I hope there are ZERO surprises at Layla Aunty's party.

GETTING READY

Thursday

I want the first party for Priya's Parties to feel official. So I had to make amazing invitations!

You are invited to:
An ORANGE SNACK party
to save the quokkas
for Layla Aunty's birthday!
365 Pine Crest Lane
12 p.m.
Saturday

Melissa and I make a good team. We have different skills, though.

ME

Kind of quiet

Pays attention to details

Loves numbers!

I know lots of fancy color names.

Scarlet

Lavender

Taupe
(rhymes with "nope")

MELISSA

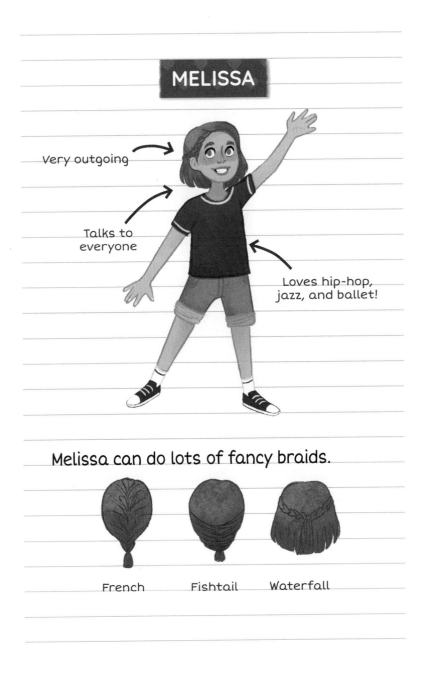

Very outgoing

Talks to everyone

Loves hip-hop, jazz, and ballet!

Melissa can do lots of fancy braids.

French   Fishtail   Waterfall

We rode our bikes around the neighborhood to deliver the invitations.

This took us a long time because I had to talk to everyone about my SUPERSECRET plan for Layla Aunty's present.

I am tired from all that biking and talking, but Melissa doesn't seem tired.

That's excellent because we still have a lot of work to do.

DIY Don't Buy Rule:

Make awesome decorations!

You don't have to spend lots of money on decorations. You can DIY them! You just need some craft supplies:

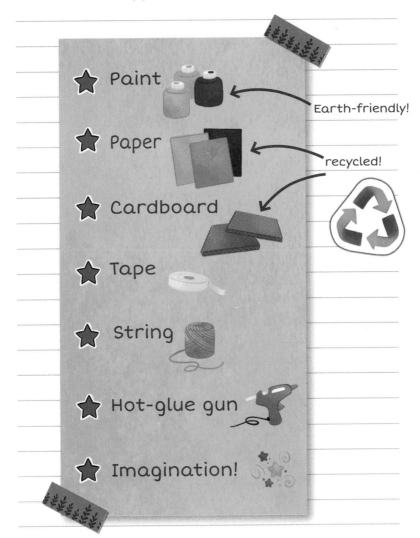

⭐ Paint

Earth-friendly!

⭐ Paper

recycled!

⭐ Cardboard

⭐ Tape

⭐ String

⭐ Hot-glue gun

⭐ Imagination!

Here are the orange DIY decorations we made for Layla Aunty's party . . .

Lots of paper chains

Sammy helped!

Flip and fold.
Flip and fold.

This is going to take a while.

Round paper fans

A "Happy Birthday, Layla Aunty" banner

My whole body is tired now.

Achy brain from thinking

Achy legs from biking

Achy fingers from crafting

I crossed TWO things off the list though.

Layla Aunty's Party To-Do List:

💜 Make and deliver invitations.

💜 Make DIY decorations.

💜 Make Layla Aunty's present.

💜 Make snacks.

But there is STILL so much to do before the party on Saturday!

Friday

I didn't sleep much last night. Layla Aunty's party is TOMORROW. I am so nervous! My insides feel like twisted-up jalebi.

I wish I didn't have to go to school today.

At breakfast, Baba wanted to talk about my business.

Tomorrow is the <u>launch</u> of Priya's Parties! If your first event goes well, I'm sure you will get more business.

Um, yeah. Thanks, Baba.

MANGO PICKLE

I can't think about planning MORE parties. I feel stressed thinking about ONE!

At least I finished Layla Aunty's present last night. Phew! I hope she likes it.

After school, I went straight to the kitchen to make snacks for the party.

Sammy mixed the chevdo.

My mom tried to be helpful, too. But she does not understand ORANGE snack party.

Should I wash some grapes?

Grapes are not orange.

Okay. Should I slice some watermelon?

Sigh.

It's hard running your own business. Especially when you have to work with family.

Dida is a champion volunteer, though. She made samosas for the party. (I helped with the filling.)

These samosas have pumpkin inside, like you wanted. Taste and tell me. What do you think?

Mmmm. They're different . . . and really good!

Susan Aunty promised to bring a box of jalebi from Rajah Sweets. That's our favorite Indian bakery. Their jalebi is the best jalebi.

Neda Aunty will bring mango lassi.

And Padma Aunty will bring food, too.

YAY! I'm done with my to-do list!

Layla Aunty's Party To-Do List:

💚 ~~Make and deliver invitations.~~

💚 ~~Make DIY decorations.~~

💚 ~~Make Layla Aunty's present.~~

💚 ~~Make snacks.~~

But I still don't feel ready . . . What am I forgetting?

Oh no! I forgot to choose my outfit for the party. Melissa is coming over to help me pick.

I tried on jeans and a T-shirt.

Then I tried on a salwar kameez (sahl-waar kum-eez).

Then I tried on jeans and an orange kurti (koor-tee).

This outfit wins! You look the most happy in it. Take lots of pictures at the party. I want to see everything!

I wish Melissa was coming to Layla Aunty's party. I will be the only kid there.

Now that I'm looking in the mirror, my heart starts beating really fast. Everything is done. But something could still go wrong.

What if the decorations don't look nice?

What if people don't like the food?

What if Layla Aunty doesn't like her party?

PARTY PREP

Saturday Morning

I woke up feeling nervous. Ma drove us to
Layla Aunty's house to set up for the party
while Layla Aunty was at the salon.

Layla is getting her hair
done for her birthday!

I thought her house would be empty, but I was surprised when we got there.

We can all help you set up, Priya.

I really wish Ma had told me the aunties would be there early. Remember how I said I don't like surprises AT ALL? I just stood there, blinking.

Then everybody's phones started buzzing.

YEEKS! That was not a lot of time! Now I'm SO glad I have extra help!

Heart pounding, I jumped into action. Usually, I don't like being in charge. But all of a sudden, I was like a boss, telling everyone how they could help.

You could hang the decorations, Padma Aunty. You're the tallest.

She's only taller in heels.

I'm an inch taller, even with bare feet.

I told Neda Aunty and Padma Aunty they could work together. The last thing I needed before the party was an Aunty Fight.

Everybody helped me set up the food table.

Neda Aunty, you can put your pitcher of mango lassi over there.

Here's the box of jalebi.

RAJAH SWEETS

I made homemade carrot cake! I learned how to do icing roses from a video on the internet.

Wow, Padma!

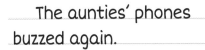

The aunties' phones buzzed again.

Layla will be here in two minutes!

I looked around Layla Aunty's living room. A paper fan had come unglued. A paper chain had fallen. I pointed around the room, and everybody scrambled to make everything just right.

Then Padma Aunty screamed.

BIRTHDAY JOY

Saturday Afternoon

I wish I'd gotten a picture of Layla Aunty's face when she first saw the living room. It was amazing, like a heart emoji in real life.

Priya, you've really done it! This is FABULOUS!

Oh, well, um . . . I had lots of help!

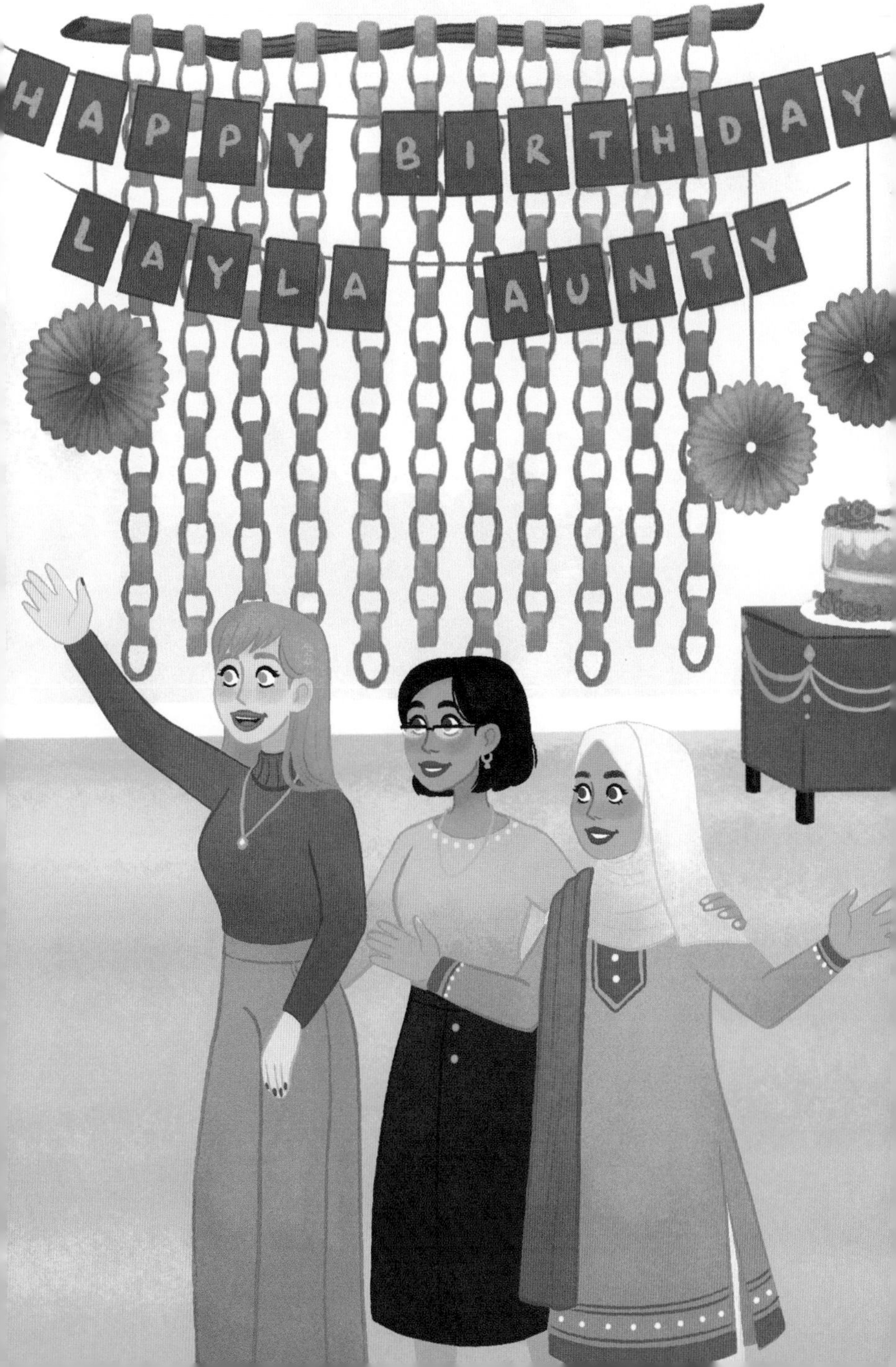
HAPPY BIRTHDAY
LAYLA AUNTY

I was the only kid at the party, so I sat in a corner and watched everyone. That's actually my favorite thing to do at parties.

Mmmm. This isn't a potato samosa. What is it?

Pumpkin! Trick or treat?

Not what I was expecting, but definitely a TREAT!

Padma Aunty put a tall orange candle on the cake.

Make a wish!

Layla Aunty blew out her candle. I smiled. The party was perfect. The food was yummy. The decorations looked amazing. People looked happy.

Now was the perfect time to give Layla Aunty the present I had made. But I suddenly felt really shy. I didn't want everybody staring at me.

I went to the bathroom and splashed water on my face. I made sure nothing was stuck in my teeth.

Then I took a deep breath and told myself, "You can do this, Priya."

THE SPECIAL SURPRISE

Saturday Late Afternoon

When Layla Aunty unwrapped my present, she laughed (in a good way!). I'd made a special book for her. Layla Aunty was laughing because I'd put a picture of SRK on the cover.

SRK stands for Shah Rukh Khan *(Shaw Rook Khaan)*. He is Layla Aunty's favorite Bollywood actor. (Bollywood is like Hollywood, but in India.) SRK stars in cheesy romantic comedies.

Famous hair!

Happy Birthday, Darling!

Starred in over 100 movies!

Dimples!

Speaks many different languages, such as English, Hindi, and Urdu!

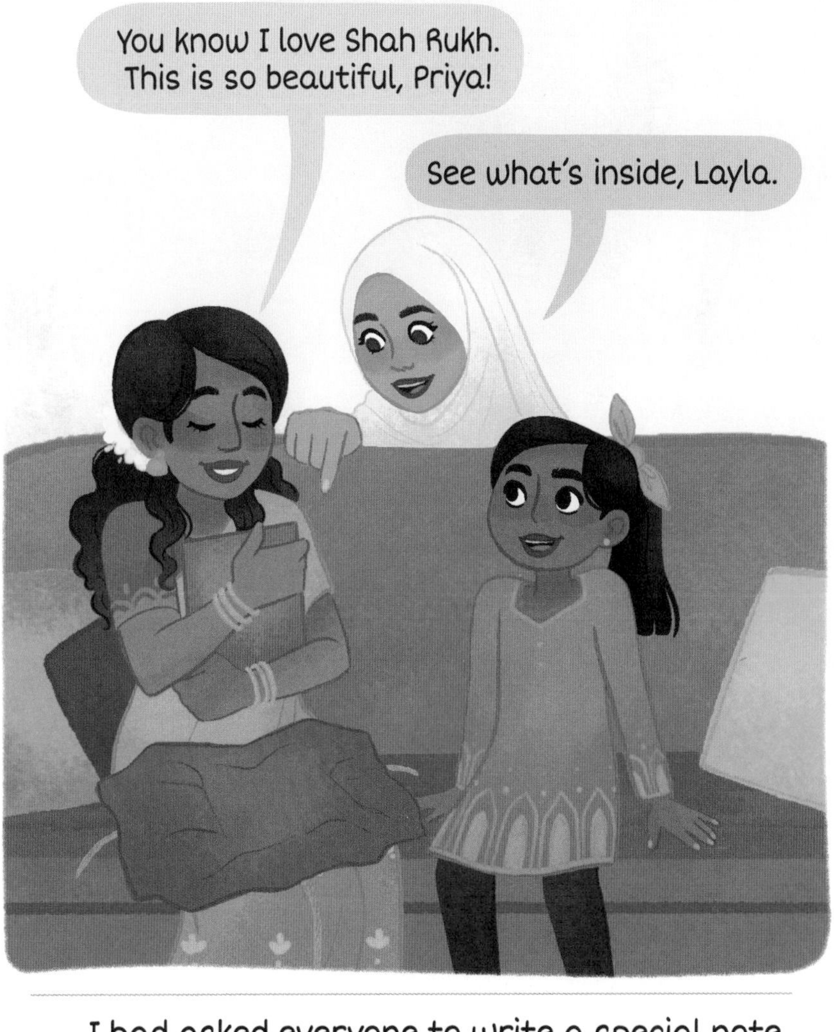
You know I love Shah Rukh. This is so beautiful, Priya!
See what's inside, Layla.

I had asked everyone to write a special note when Melissa and I delivered the invitations. Then I put them all together in this book . . .

Happy Birthday, Layla!
Life would be boring without your wild ideas.
I will always remember that day at the zoo.
I think the elephant will, too.
Elephants never forget.
Love,
Susan

Layla, you never take your foot off the gas. I love our adventures. Even if we sometimes end up in the lake . . .
All the best!
Neda

Darling, nothing rhymes with orange. It's quite special, Like you. Love, Padma

60

Layla, dearest friend,
have a spectacular day.
Lots of love, Reeta

Dear Layla Aunty,
I hope you liked your party.
You're a very special person.
Happy birthday!
Love,
Priya

Layla Aunty started crying. When other people cry, it makes me start crying, too.

Thank you for putting all of this together.

You're welcome, Layla Aunty. You can use the rest of the pages like a diary. Happy birthday!

I thought the book was going to be the big surprise. But there was one more REALLY BIG surprise. And this time, it was for me!

THE REALLY BIG SURPRISE

Saturday Evening

I know I said I don't like surprises, but I REALLY liked this one.

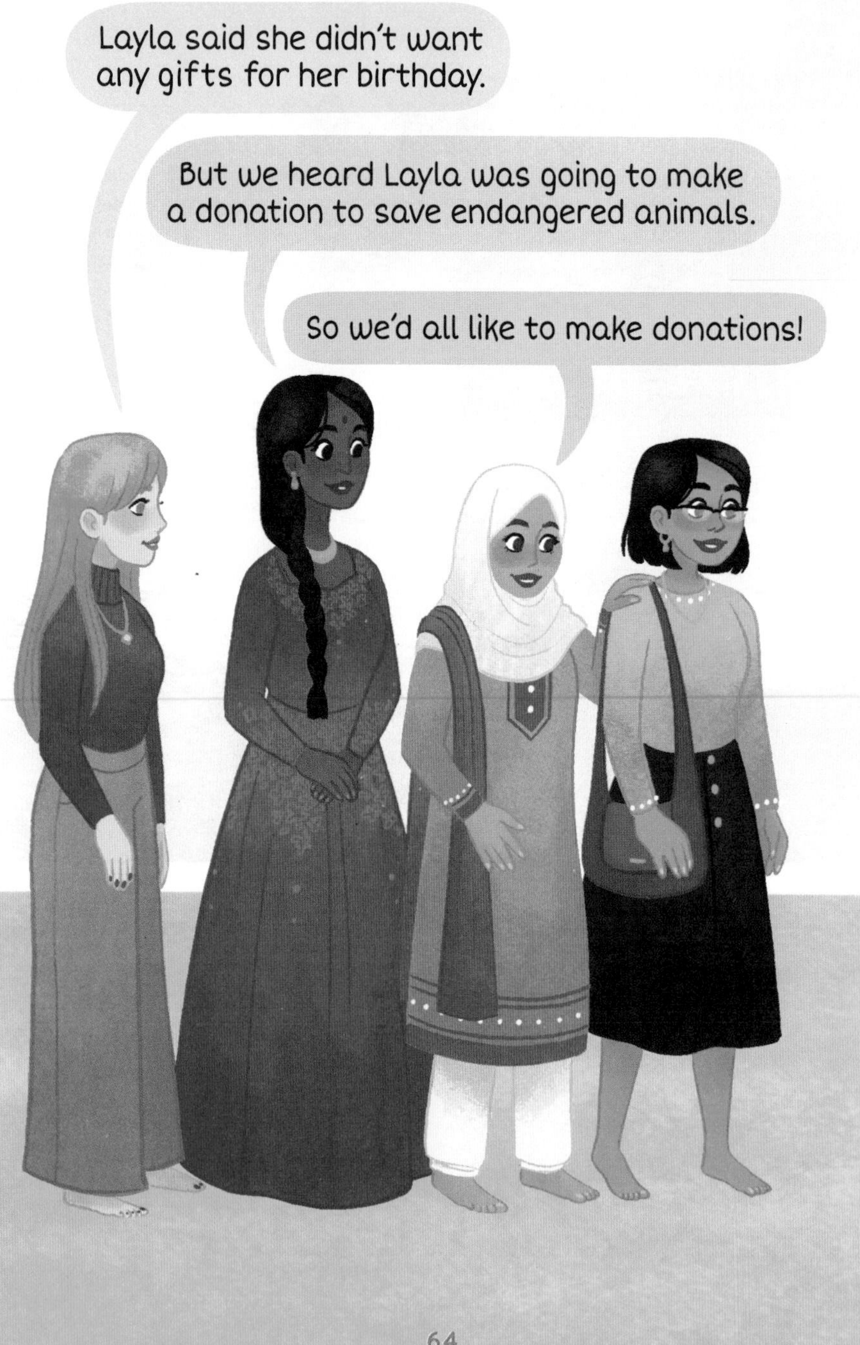
Layla said she didn't want any gifts for her birthday.
But we heard Layla was going to make a donation to save endangered animals.
So we'd all like to make donations!

I just stood like a statue, staring at everybody. I think my mouth was hanging open. I didn't know what to say.

HOW I'M FEELING

Surprised (obviously)

Happy

Overwhelmed (like
I might start crying
again)

After more talking and snacking, I said
thank you and gave everybody hugs.

Layla Aunty told us not to clean up. She wanted to keep the decorations up for a little bit longer.

This is my favorite birthday yet! Thanks to all of you—and especially Priya's Parties!

I am so proud of my new business. I feel really good doing what I love—DIY crafts, making people happy, and helping animals.

When I got home, I designed a logo. Here it is:

I also came up with a slogan, which is a fun way to help people remember what my business does:

Helping the planet,
one AWESOME party
at a time.

It's catchy, right?

Sunday

Baba helped me send the party money to a group that helps quokkas.

Your donation will help protect quokkas and the places they live. Well done, Priya.

I can't wait to find the next animal to help with Priya's Parties!

I posted pictures from Layla Aunty's Awesome Orange Birthday.

Priya Chakraborty

Planned this party for my aunty. Can you guess her favorite color?

Ethan Jackman

Orange? 😋

Melissa Williams

YAY! It looks so fun! 😄

Reeta Chakraborty

So proud of you! It was
a great party! Love, Ma. 🫖

Tara Singh

Hi, Priya! I'm Layla Aunty's niece.
We've actually met a few times.
This party looks AMAZING. Could
Priya's Parties plan a party for
me and my friends? 🎭

Yeeks and yay? Time to plan another party!

DIY YOUR PARTY!
PAPER-CHAIN CURTAIN

Make a fun, simple wall hanging that works as a decoration or photo backdrop.

WHAT YOU'LL NEED

- Construction paper
- Scissors
- Glue, sticky tape, or a stapler
- Long stick
- String, wire, or hooks

GET STARTED

1. To make a 3 foot by 4 foot paper-chain curtain, cut your paper into strips that are 1 to 1-1/2 inches wide and 6 to 8 inches tall. When you have two strips ready, move on to step 2.

2. Make the first loop of a chain: Take one strip of paper and curl it into a loop so the two ends meet. Glue, tape, or staple the ends together so that one strip makes a circle.

3. Feed your second strip of paper through the middle of the loop you just made. Curl the new strip into a loop so the two ends meet. Connect the ends. You have completed the first two loops of your first chain!

4. Cut more strips. Repeat step 3 until you have a long chain of about 20 paper loops. Then you have completed your first chain!

5. Make more chains! Try to make at least 10 paper chains. The chains can be different lengths, colors, and sizes. Be creative!

6. Once all your chains are ready, slide the first loop of each chain onto the long stick. This will create a curtain of paper chains.

PARTY TIME

Use string, wire, or hooks to hang your curtain. Take and share selfies with your finished party decoration!

1 Priya shares five facts about quokkas on page 6. Do some research! Can you come up with two new facts?

2 Making to-do lists can be a great way to keep track of things you need to do. Can you name all the items on Priya's to-do list?

3 Surprises make Priya feel nervous. Why? How do you feel about surprises?

4 On page 30, Priya feels tired all over. Even her brain aches "from thinking." What kinds of things make your brain feel achy or tired?

5 A haiku is a poem that was invented in Japan. It has three lines of text. Each line has a specific number of syllables: five, seven, and five. There are two haiku poems on pages 60–61. Find them! Then write your own!

ABOUT THE CREATORS

Mitali Banerjee Ruths grew up in Texas and was a LOT like Priya when she was younger. She wanted to start a business, save the planet, and help endangered animals.

Mitali now lives in Canada. She still cares about animals, protecting the environment, and finding ways to be a better earthling. Someday, she wants to visit Australia and meet a quokka.

↖ Mitali's sister met a quokka!

Aaliya Jaleel loves illustrating books with bright, bold color palettes and exciting, lovable characters. When she is not drawing, she's planning fun parties that never quite go as planned—but that turn out memorable nonetheless.

Aaliya currently lives in Texas with her husband. She loves exploring and finding hidden treasures when traveling to new places.

The Party Diaries

Read more books!

The Party Diaries
BRANCHES
Starry Henna Night
written by
Mitali Banerjee Ruths
art by
Aaliya Jaleel
SCHOLASTIC

2

The Party Diaries
BRANCHES
Top Secret Anniversary
written by
Mitali Banerjee Ruths
art by
Aaliya Jaleel
SCHOLASTIC

3

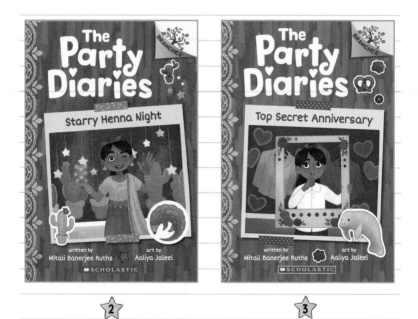